D1225921

The Modern Art of
TAMING
WILD
HORSES

5.

s

The Modern Art of
TAMING WILD HORSES

BY
J.S. Rarey
The American Horse Tamer

APPLEWOOD BOOKS

BEDFORD, MASSACHUSETTS

The Modern Art of Taming Wild Horses was originally published in 1856.

636.10886
R182

ISBN 1-55709-126-9

Thank you for purchasing an Applewood Book.
Applewood reprints America's lively classics—books
from the past that are of interest to modern readers.
For a free copy of our current catalog, write to:
Applewood Books, 18 North Road, Bedford,
Massachusetts 01730.

10 9 8 7 6 5 4 3 2 1

Library of Congress Cataloging-in-Publication Data
Rarey, J. S. (John Solomon), 1827-1866.
  The Modern art of taming wild horses / by J. S.
Rarey.
        p.   cm.
  Originally published: Columbus: Ohio State
Journal Co., 1856.
  ISBN 1-55709-126-9
  1. Horses—Training.   I. Title.
SF287.R246   1995
636.1'0886–dc20   95-36386
                                              CIP

KENT FREE LIBRARY

CONTENTS

TAMING OF WILD HORSES

By J. S. RAREY,
THE AMERICAN HORSE TAMER.

THE THREE FUNDAMENTAL PRINCIPLES OF MY THEORY;
Founded on the Leading Characteristics of the Horse.

FIRST—That he is so constituted by nature that he will not offer resistance to any demand made of him which he fully comprehends, if made in a way consistent with the laws of his nature.

SECOND—That he has no consciousness of his strength beyond his experience, and can be handled according to our will without force.

THIRD—That we can, in compliance with the laws of his nature by which he examines all things new to him, take any object, however frightful, around, over, or on him, that does not inflict pain, without causing him to fear.

To take these assertions in order, I will first give you some of the reasons why I think he is naturally obedient, and will not offer resistance to anything fully comprehended. The horse, though possessed of some faculties superior to man's, being deficient in reasoning powers, has no knowledge of right or wrong, of free will and independent government, and knows not of any imposition practised upon him, however unreasonable these impositions may be. Consequently, he cannot come to any decision as to what he should or should not do, because he has not the reasoning faculties of man to argue the justice of the thing demanded of him. If he had, taking into consideration his superior strength, he would be useless to man as a servant. Give him mind in proportion to his strength, and he will demand of us the green fields for his inheritance, where he will roam at leisure, denying the right of servitude at all. God has wisely formed his nature so that it can be operated upon by the knowledge of man according to the dictates of his will; and he might well be termed an unconscious, submissive servant. This truth we can see verified in every day's experience by the abuses practised upon him. Any one who chooses to be so cruel, can mount the noble steed and run him till he drops with fatigue, or, as is often the case with the more spirited, falls dead beneath his rider. If he had the power to reason, would he not rear and pitch his rider, rather than suffer him to run him to death? Or would he condescend to carry at all the vain impostor, who, with but equal intellect, was trying to impose on his equal rights and equally independent spirit? But happily for us, he has no consciousness of imposition, no thought of disobedience except by impulse caused by the violation of the law of his nature. Consequently, when disobedient, it is the fault of man.

Then, we can but come to the conclusion that, if a horse is not taken in a way at variance with the laws of his nature, he will do anything that he fully comprehends, without making any offer of resistance.

Second—The fact of the horse being unconscious of the amount of his strength can be proven to the satisfaction of any one. For instance, such remarks as these are common, and perhaps familiar to your recollection. One person says to another, "If that wild horse there was conscious of the amount of his strength, his owner would have no business with him in that vehicle; such light reins and harness too—if he knew he could snap them asunder in a minute and be as free as the air we breathe;" and, "That horse yonder, that is pawing and fretting to follow the company that is fast leaving him—if he knew his strength, he would not remain long fastened to that hitching post so much against his will, by a strap that would no more resist his powerful weight and strength than a cotton thread would bind a strong man." Yet these facts, made common by every-day occurrence, are not thought of as anything wonderful. Like the ignorant man who looks at the different phases of the moon, you look at these things as he looks at her different changes without troubling your mind with the question, "Why are these things so?" What would be the condition of the world if all our minds lay dormant? If men did not think, reason, and act, our undisturbed, slumbering intellects would not excel the imbecility of the brute; we should live in chaos, hardly aware of our existence. And yet, with all our activity of mind, we daily pass by unobserved that which would be wonderful if philosophized and reasoned upon; and with the same inconsistency wonder at that which a little consideration, reason, and philosophy would make but a simple affair.

Third—He will allow any object, however frightful in appearance, to come around, over, or on him, that does not inflict pain.

We know from a natural course of reasoning,

that there has never been an effect without a cause, and we infer from this, that there can be no action either in animate or inanimate matter, without there first being some cause to produce it. And from this self-evident fact we know that there is some cause for every impulse or movement of either mind or matter, and that this law governs every action or movement of the animal kingdom. Then, according to this theory, there must be some cause before fear can exist; and, if fear exists from the effect of imagination, and not from the infliction of real pain, it can be removed by complying with those laws of nature by which the horse examines an object, and determines upon its innocence or harm.

A log or stump by the road side may be, in the imagination of the horse, some great beast about to pounce upon him; but after you take him up to it and let him stand by it a little while, and touch it with his nose, and go through his process of examination, he will not care anything more about it. And the same principle and process will have the same effect with any other object, however frightful in appearance, in which there is no harm. Take a boy that has been frightened by a false face, or any other object that he could not comprehend at once; but let him take that face, or object in his hands and examine it, and he will not care anything more about it. This is a demonstration of the same principle.

With this introduction to the principles of my theory, I shall next attempt to teach you how to put it into practice; and, whatever instructions may follow you can rely on, as having been proven practically by my own experiments. And knowing from experience just what obstacles I have met with in handling bad horses, I shall try to anticipate them for you, and assist you in surmounting them, by commencing with the first steps to be taken with the colt, and accompany you through the whole task of breaking.

HOW TO SUCCEED IN GETTING THE COLT FROM PASTURE.

Go to the pasture and walk around the whole herd quietly, and at such a distance as not to cause them to scare and run. Then approach them very slowly, and if they stick up their heads and seem to be frightened, wait until they become quiet, so as not to make them run before you are close enough to drive them in the direction you want them to go. And when you begin to drive, do not flourish your arms or halloo, but gently follow them off, leaving the direction free for them that you wish them to take. Thus taking advantage of their ignorance, you will be able to get them into the pound as easily as the hunter drives the quails into his net. For, if they have always run in the pasture uncared for (as many horses do in prairie countries and on large plantations), there is no reason why they should not be as wild as the sportsman's birds, and require the same gentle treatment, if you want to get them without trouble; for the horse in his natural state, is as wild as any of the undomesticated animals, though more easily tamed than the most of them.

How to Stable a Colt without Trouble.

The next step will be, to get the horse into a stable or shed. This should be done as quietly as possible, so as not to excite any suspicion in the horse of any danger befalling him. The best way to do this, is to lead a gentle horse into the stable first, and hitch him, then quietly walk around the colt and let him go in of his own accord. It is almost impossible to get men who have never practised on this principle to go slowly and considerately enough about it. They do not know that in handling a wild horse, above all other things, is that good old adage true, that "haste makes waste;" that is, waste of time—for the gain of trouble and perplexity.

One wrong move may frighten your horse, and make him think it necessary to escape at all hazards for the safety of his life—and thus make two hours' work of a ten minutes' job; and this would be all your own fault, and entirely unnecessary—for he will not run unless you run after him, and that would not be good policy unless you knew that you could outrun him, for you will have to let him stop of his own accord after all. But he will not try to break away unless you attempt to force him into measures. If he does not see the way at once, and is a little fretful about going in, do not undertake to drive him, but give him a little less room outside, by gently closing in around him. Do not raise your arms, but let them hang at your side, for you might as well raise a club: the horse has never studied anatomy, and does not know but that they will unhinge themselves and fly at him. If he attempts to turn back, walk before him, but do not run; and if he gets past you, encircle him again in the same quiet manner, and he will soon find that you are not going to hurt him; and then you can walk so close around him that he will go into the stable for more room, and to get farther from you. As soon as he is in, remove the quiet horse and shut the door. This will be his first notion of confinement—not knowing how he got into such a place, nor

how to get out of it. That he may take it as quietly as possible, see that the shed is entirely free
from dogs, chickens, or anything that would
annoy him. Then give him a few ears of corn, and
let him remain alone fifteen or twenty minutes,
until he has examined his apartment, and has
become reconciled to his confinement.

TIME TO REFLECT.

And now, while your horse is eating those
few ears of corn, is the proper time to see that
your halter is ready and all right, and to reflect on
the best mode of operations; for in horsebreaking
it is highly important that you should be gov-
erned by some system. And you should know,
before you attempt to do anything, just what you
are going to do, and how you are going to do it.
And, if you are experienced in the art of taming
wild horses, you ought to be able to tell, within a
few minutes, the length of time it would take you
to halter the colt, and teach him to lead.

THE KIND OF HALTER.

Always use a leather halter, and be sure to
have it made so that it will not draw tight around
his nose if he pulls on it. It should be of the right

size to fit his head easily and nicely; so that the nose-band will not be too tight or too low. Never put a rope halter on an unbroken colt, under any circumstances whatever. They have caused more horses to hurt or kill themselves than would pay for twice the cost of all the leather halters that have ever been needed for the purpose of haltering colts. It is almost impossible to break a colt that is very wild with a rope halter, without having him pull, rear, and throw himself, and thus endanger his life; and I will tell you why. It is just as natural for a horse to try to get his head out of anything that hurts it, or feels unpleasant, as it would be for you to try to get your hand out of a fire. The cords of the rope are hard and cutting; this makes him raise his head and draw on it, and as soon as he pulls, the slip noose (the way rope halters are always made) tightens, and pinches his nose, and then he will struggle for life, until, perchance, he throws himself; and who would have his horse throw himself, and run the risk of breaking his neck, rather than pay the price of a leather halter? But this is not the worst. A horse that has once pulled on his halter can never be as well broken as one that has never pulled at all.

REMARKS ON THE HORSE.

But before we attempt to do anything more with the colt, I will give you some of the characteristics of his nature, that you may better understand his motions. Every one that has ever paid any attention to the horse, has noticed his natural inclination to smell everything which to him looks new and frightful. This is their strange mode of examining everything. And, when they are frightened at anything, though they look at it sharply, they seem to have no confidence in this optical examination alone, but must touch it with the nose before they are entirely satisfied; and, as soon as this is done, all is right.

EXPERIMENT WITH THE ROBE.

If you want to satisfy yourself of this characteristic of the horse, and to learn something of importance concerning the peculiarities of his nature, etc., turn him into the barn-yard, or a large stable will do, and then gather up something that you know will frighten him—a red blanket, buffalo-robe, or something of that kind. Hold it up so that he can see it; he will stick up his head and snort. Then throw it down somewhere in the centre of the lot or barn, and walk off to one side.

Watch his motions, and study his nature. If he is frightened at the object, he will not rest until he has touched it with his nose. You will see him begin to walk around the robe and snort, all the time getting a little closer, as if drawn up by some magic spell, until he finally gets within reach of it. He will then very cautiously stretch out his neck as far as he can reach, merely touching it with his nose, as though he thought it was ready to fly at him. But after he has repeated these touches a few times, for the first time (though he has been looking at it all the while) he seems to have an idea what it is. But now he has found, by the sense of feeling, that it is nothing that will do him any harm, and he is ready to play with it. And if you watch him closely, you will see him take hold of it with his teeth, and raise it up and pull at it. And in a few minutes you can see that he has not that same wild look about his eye, but stands like a horse biting at some familiar stump.

Yet the horse is never so well satisfied when he is about anything that has frightened him, as when he is standing with his nose to it. And, in nine cases out of ten, you will see some of that same wild look about him again, as he turns to walk from it. And you will probably see him looking back very suspiciously as he walks away, as though he thought it might come after him yet.

And in all probability, he will have to go back and make another examination before he is satisfied. But he will familiarize himself with it, and, if he should run in that lot a few days, the robe that frightened him so much at first will be no more to him than a familiar stump.

―――――

Suggestions on the Habit of Smelling.

We might very naturally suppose from the fact of the horse's applying his nose to everything new to him, that he always does so for the purpose of smelling these objects; but I believe that it is as much or more for the purpose of feeling, and that he makes use of his nose, or muzzle (as it is sometimes called), as we would of our hands; because it is the only organ by which he can touch or feel anything with much susceptibility.

I believe that he invariably makes use of the four senses—seeing, hearing, smelling, and feeling—in all of his examinations, of which the sense of feeling is, perhaps, the most important. And I think that, in the experiment with the robe, his gradual approach and final touch with his nose was as much for the purpose of feeling as anything else, his sense of smell being so keen that it would not be necessary for him to touch his nose against anything in order to get the proper scent;

for it is said that a horse can smell a man at the distance of a mile. And if the scent of the robe was all that was necessary, he could get that several rods off. But we know from experience, that if a horse sees and smells a robe a short distance from him, he is very much frightened (unless he is used to it) until he touches it with his nose; which is a positive proof that feeling is the controlling sense in this case.

———

PREVAILING OPINION OF HORSEMEN.

It is a prevailing opinion among horsemen generally that the sense of smell is the governing sense of the horse. And Faucher, as well as others, has with that view got up receipts of strong smelling oils, etc., to tame the horse, sometimes using the chestnut of his leg, which they dry, grind into powder, and blow into his nostrils, sometimes using the oils of rhodium, origanum, etc., that are noted for their strong smell; and sometimes they scent the hand with the sweat from under the arm, or blow their breath into his nostrils, etc., etc. All of which, as far as the scent goes, have no effect whatever in gentling the horse, or conveying any idea to his mind; though the acts that accompany these efforts—handling him, touching him about the nose and head, and patting him, as they direct you should, after administering the articles, may have a very great effect, which they mistake to be the effect of the ingredients used. And Faucher, in his work, entitled "The Arabian Art of Taming Horses," page 17, tells us how to accustom a horse to a robe, by administering certain articles to his nose; and goes on to say that these articles must first be applied to the horse's nose before you attempt to break him, in order to operate successfully.

Now, reader, can you, or any one else, give one single reason how scent can convey any idea to the horse's mind of what we want him to do? If not, then of course strong scents of any kind are of no avail in taming the unbroken horse. For, everything that we get him to do of his own accord, without force, must be accomplished by some means of conveying our ideas to his mind. I say to my horse, "Go-'long!" and he goes. "Ho!" and he stops; because these two words, of which he has learned the meaning by the tap of the whip and the pull of the rein that first accompanied them, convey the two ideas to his mind of go and stop.

Neither Faucher, nor any one else, can ever teach the horse a single thing by the means of scent alone.

How long do you suppose a horse would

have to stand and smell a bottle of oil before he would learn to bend his knee and make a bow at your bidding, "Go yonder and bring your hat," or "Come here and lie down"? Thus you see the absurdity of trying to break or tame the horse by the means of receipts for articles to smell at, or medicine to give him, of any kind whatever.

The only science that has ever existed in the world, relative to the breaking of horses, that has been of any value, is that true method which takes them in their native state, and improves their intelligence.

POWEL'S SYSTEM OF APPROACHING THE COLT.

But, before we go further, I will give you Willis J. Powel's system of approaching a wild colt, as given by him in a work on the "Art of Taming Wild Horses." He says, "A horse is gentled by my secret in from two to sixteen hours." The time I have most commonly employed has been from four to six hours.

REMARKS ON POWEL'S TREATMENT.—HOW TO GOVERN HORSES OF ANY KIND.

These instructions are very good, but not quite sufficient for horses of all kinds, and for haltering and leading the colt; but I have inserted them here because they give some of the true philosophy of approaching the horse, and of establishing confidence between man and horse. He speaks only of the kind that fear man.

To those who understand the philosophy of horsemanship, these are the easiest trained; for when we have a horse that is wild and lively, we can train him to our will in a very short time—for they are generally quick to learn, and always ready to obey. But there is another kind that are of a stubborn or vicious disposition; and although they are not wild, and do not require taming in the sense it is generally understood, they are just as ignorant as a wild horse, if not more so, and need to be taught just as much: and in order to have them obey quickly, it is very necessary that they should be made to fear their master; for, in order to obtain perfect obedience from any horse, we must first have him fear us, for our motto is, fear, love, and obey; and we must have the fulfillment of the first two before we can expect the latter; for it is by our philosophy of creating fear, love, and confidence, that we govern to our will every kind of horse whatever.

Then, in order to take horses as we find them, of all kinds, and to train them to our liking, we will always take with us, when we go into a stable to train a colt, a long switch whip (whalebone buggy-whips are the best), with a good silk cracker, so as to cut keenly and make a sharp report, which, if handled with dexterity, and rightly applied, accompanied with a sharp fierce word, will be sufficient to enliven the spirits of any horse. With this whip in your right hand, with the lash pointing backward, enter the stable alone. It is a great disadvantage in training a horse to have any one in the stable with you; you should be entirely alone, so as to have nothing but yourself to attract his attention. If he is wild, you will soon see him on the opposite side of the stable from you; and now is the time to use a little judgment. I should not want, for myself, more than half or three-quarters of an hour to handle any kind of a colt, and have him running about in the stable after me; though I would advise a new beginner to take more time, and not be in too much of a hurry. If you have but one colt to gentle, and are not particular about the length of time you spend, and have not had any experience in handling colts, I would advise you to take Mr. Powel's method at first, till you gentle him, which he says takes from two to six hours. But as I want to accomplish the same, and what is more, teach the horse to lead, in less than one hour, I shall give you a much quicker process of accomplishing the same end. Accordingly, when you have entered the stable, stand still, and let your horse look at you a minute or two, and as soon as he is settled in one place, approach him slowly, with both arms stationary, your right hanging by your side, holding the whip as directed and the left bent at the elbow, with your hand projecting. As you approach him, go not too much towards his head or croup, so as not to make him move either forward or backward, thus keeping your horse stationary; if he does move a little either forward or backward, step a little to the right or left very cautiously; this will keep him in one place. As you get very near him, draw a little to his shoulder, and stop a few seconds. If you are in his reach he will turn his head and smell your hand, not that he has any preference for your hand, but because that is projecting, and is the nearest portion of your body to the horse. This all colts will do, and they will smell your naked hand just as quickly as they will anything that you can put in it, and with just as good an effect, however much some men have preached the doctrine of taming horses by giving them the scent of articles from the hand. I have already proved that to be a mistake. As soon as he touches his nose to your hand, caress him as before directed, always using a very light soft hand, merely touching the horse, always rubbing the way the hair lies, so that your hand will pass along as smoothly as possible. As you stand by his side, you may find it more convenient to rub his neck or the side of his head, which will answer the same purpose as rubbing his forehead. Favour every inclination of the horse to smell or touch you with his nose. Always follow each touch or communication of this kind with the most tender and affectionate caresses, accompanied with a kind look, and pleasant word of some sort, such as, "Ho! my little boy—ho! my little boy!" "Pretty boy!" "Nice lady!" or something of that kind, constantly repeating the same words, with the same kind, steady tone of voice; for the horse soon learns to read the expression of the face and voice, and will know as well when fear, love, or anger prevails, as you know your own feelings; two of which, fear and anger, a good horseman should never feel.

How to Proceed if Your Horse Be of a Stubborn Disposition.

If your horse, instead of being wild, seems to be of a stubborn or mulish disposition; if he lays back his ears as you approach him, or turns his heels to kick you, he has not that regard or fear of man that he should have, to enable you to handle him quickly and easily; and it might be well to give him a few sharp cuts with the whip, about the legs, pretty close to the body. It will crack keenly as it plies around his legs, and the crack of the whip will affect him as much as the stroke; besides, one sharp cut about his legs will affect him more than two or three over his back, the skin on the inner part of his legs or about his flank being thinner, more tender, than on his back. But do not whip him much—just enough to scare him; it is not because we want to hurt the horse that we whip him, we only do it to scare that bad disposition out of him. But whatever you do, do quickly, sharply, and with a good deal of fire, but always without anger. If you are going to scare him at all you must do it at once. Never go into a pitched battle with your horse, and whip him until he is mad and will fight you; you had better not touch him at all, for you will establish, instead of fear and regard, feelings of resentment, hatred, and ill-will. It will do him no good, but an injury, to strike a blow, unless you can scare him; but if you succeed in scaring him, you can whip him without making him mad; for fear and anger never exist together in the horse, and as soon as one is visible, you will find that the other has disappeared. As soon as you have frightened him so that he will stand up straight and pay some attention to you, approach him again, and caress him a good deal more than you whipped him, then you will excite the two controlling passions of his nature, love and fear, and then he will love and fear you too, and, as soon as he learns what to do, will obey quickly.

How to Halter and Lead a Colt.

As soon as you have gentled the colt a little, take the halter in your left hand and approach him as before, and on the same side that you have gentled him. If he is very timid about your approaching closely to him, you can get up to him quicker by making the whip a part of your arm, and reaching out very gently with the butt-end of it; rubbing him lightly on the neck, all the time getting a little closer, shortening the whip by taking it up in your hand, until you finally get close enough to put your hands on him. If he is inclined to hold his head from you, put the end of the halter-strap around his neck, drop your whip, and draw very gently; he will let his neck give, and you can pull his head to you. Then take hold of that part of the halter which buckles over the top of his head, and pass the long side, or that part which goes into the buckle, under his neck, grasping it on the opposite side with your right

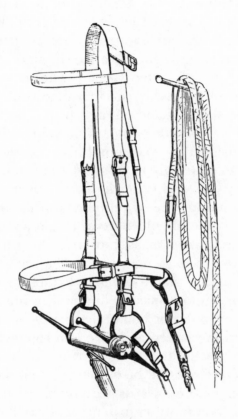

HALTER AND BRIDLE FOR COLTS.

hand, letting the first strap loose—the latter will be sufficient to hold his head to you. Lower the halter a little, just enough to get his nose into that part which goes around it; then raise it somewhat, and fasten the top buckle, and you will have it all right. The first time you halter a colt you should stand on the left side, pretty well back to his shoulder, only taking hold of that part of the halter that goes round his neck; then with your two hands about his neck you can hold his head to you, and raise the halter on it without making him dodge by putting your hands about his nose. You should have a long rope or strap ready, and as soon as you have the halter on, attach this to it, so that you can let him walk the length of the stable without letting go of the strap, or without making him pull on the halter, for if you only let him feel the weight of your hand on the halter, and give him rope when he runs from you, he will never rear, pull, or throw himself, yet you will be holding him all the time, and doing more towards gentling him than if you had the power to snub him right up and hold him to one spot; because, he does not know anything about his strength, and if you don't do anything to make him pull, he will never know that he can. In a few minutes you can begin to control him with the halter, then shorten the distance between yourself and the horse by taking up the strap in your hand.

As soon as he will allow you to hold him by a tolerably short strap, and to step up to him without flying back, you can begin to give some idea about leading. But to do this, do not go before and attempt to pull him after you, but commence by pulling him very quietly to one side. He has nothing to brace either side of his neck, and will soon yield to a steady, gradual pull of the halter; and as soon as you have pulled him a step or two to one side, step up to him and caress him, and then pull him again, repeating this operation until you can pull him around in every direction, and walk about the stable with him, which you can do in a few minutes, for he will soon think when you have made him step to the right or left a few times, that he is compelled to follow the pull of the halter, not knowing that he has the power to resist your pulling; besides you have handled him so gently that he is not afraid of you, and you always caress him when he comes up to you, and he likes that, and would just as lief follow you as not. And after he has had a few lessons of that kind, if you turn him out in a lot, he will come up to you every opportunity he gets. You should lead him about in the stable some time before you take him out, opening the door, so that he can see out, leading him up to it and back again, and past it. See that there is nothing on the outside to make him jump when you take him out, and as you go out with him, try to make him go very slowly, catching hold of the halter close to the jaw with your left hand, while the right is resting on the top of the neck, holding to his mane. After you are out with him a little while, you can lead him about as you please. Don't let any second person come up to you when you first take him out; a stranger taking hold of the halter would frighten him, and make him run. There should not even be any one standing near him, to attract his attention or scare him. If you are alone, and manage him rightly, it will not require any more force to lead or hold him than it would to manage a broken horse.

How to Lead a Colt by the Side of a Broken Horse.

If you should want to lead your colt by the side of another horse, as is often the case, I would advise you to take your horse into the stable, attach a second strap to the colt's halter, and lead your horse up alongside of him. Then get on the broken horse and take one strap around his breast, under his martingale (if he has any on), holding it in your left hand. This will prevent the colt from getting back too far; besides, you will have more power to hold him with the strap pulling against the horse's breast. The other strap take up in your right hand to prevent him from running ahead; then turn him about a few times in the stable, and if the door is wide enough, ride out with him in that position; if not, take the broken horse out first, and stand his breast up against the door, then lead the colt to the same spot, and take the straps as before directed, one on each side of his neck, then let some one start the colt out, and as he comes out, turn your horse to the left, and you will have them all right. This is the best way to lead a colt; you can manage any kind of colt in this way, without any trouble; for if he tries to run ahead, or pull back, the two straps will bring the horses facing each other, so that you can very easily follow up his movements without doing much holding, and as soon as he stops running backward you are right with him, and all ready to go ahead; and if he gets stubborn and does not want to go, you can remove all his stubbornness by riding your horse against his neck, thus compelling him to turn to the right; and as soon as you have turned him about a few times, he will be willing to go along. The next thing, after you have got through leading him, will be to take him into a stable, and hitch him in such a way as not to have him pull on the halter, and as they are often troublesome to get into a stable the first few times, I will give you some instructions about getting him in.

How to Lead a Colt into the Stable and Hitch Him without Having Him Pull on the Halter.

You should lead the broken horse into the stable first, and get the colt, if you can, to follow in after him. If he refuses to go, step up to him, taking a little stick or switch in your right hand; then take hold of the halter close to his head with your left hand, at the same time reaching over his back with your right arm, so that you can tap him on the opposite side with your switch; bring him up facing the door, tap him lightly with your switch, reaching as far back with it as you can. This tapping, by being pretty well back, and on the opposite side, will drive him ahead, and keep him close to you; then, by giving him the right direction with your left hand you can walk into the stable with him. I have walked colts into the stable in this way in less than a minute, after men had worked at them half an hour, trying to pull them in. If you cannot walk him in at once in this way, turn him about and walk him around in every direction, until you can get him up to the door without pulling at him. Then let him stand a few minutes, keeping his head in the right direction with the halter, and he will walk in in less than ten minutes. Never attempt to pull the colt into the stable; that would make him think at once that it was a dangerous place, and if he was not afraid of it before he would be then. Besides, we do not want him to know anything about pulling on the halter. Colts are often hurt, and sometimes killed, by trying to force them into the stable; and those who attempt to do it in that way go into an uphill business, when a plain smooth road is before them.

If you want to hitch your colt, put him in a tolerably wide stall, which should not be too long, and should be connected by a bar or something of that kind to the partition behind it; so that, after the colt is in, he cannot get far enough back to take a straight, backward pull on the halter; then, by hitching him in the centre of the stall, it would be impossible for him to pull on the halter, the partition behind preventing him from going back, and the halter in the centre checking him every time he turns to the right or left. In a stall of this kind you can break any horse to stand hitched by a light strap, anywhere, without his ever knowing anything about pulling. But if you have broken your horse to lead, and have learned him the use of the halter (which you should always do before you hitch him to anything), you can hitch him in any kind of a stall, and give him something to eat to keep him up to his place for a few minutes at first, and there is not one colt in fifty that will pull on his halter.

THE KIND OF BIT, AND HOW TO ACCUSTOM A HORSE TO IT.

You should use a large, smooth, snaffle-bit, so as not to hurt his mouth, with a bar to each side, to prevent the bit from pulling through either way. This you should attach to the head-stall of your bridle, and put it on your colt without any reins to it, and let him run loose in a large stable or shed some time, until he becomes a little used to the bit, and will bear it without trying to get it out of his mouth. It would be well, if convenient, to repeat this several times, before you do any-thing more with the colt; as soon as he will bear the bit, attach a single rein to it, without any mar-tingale. You should also have a halter on your colt, or a bridle made after the fashion of a halter, with a strap to it, so that you can hold or lead him about without pulling on the bit much. He is now ready for the saddle.

How to Saddle a Colt.

Any one man who understands this theory can put a saddle on the wildest colt that ever grew, without any help, and without scaring him. The first thing will be to tie each stirrup-strap into a loose knot to make them short, and prevent the stirrups from flying about and hitting him. Then double up the skirts, and take the saddle under your right arm, so as not to frighten him with it as you approach. When you get to him, rub him gently a few times with your hand, and then raise the saddle very slowly, until he can see it, and smell it, and feel it with his nose. Then let the skirt loose, and rub it very gently against his neck the way the hair lies, letting him hear the rattle of the skirts as he feels them against him — each time getting a little farther backward, and finally slip it over his shoulders on his back. Shake it a little with your hand, and in less than five minutes you can rattle it about over his back as much as you please, and pull it off and throw it on again, without his paying much attention to it.

As soon as you have accustomed him to the saddle, fasten the girth. Be careful how you do this. It often frightens the colt when he feels the girth binding him, and making the saddle fit tight on his back. You should bring up the girth very gently, and not draw it too tight at first, just enough to hold the saddle on. Move him a little, and then girth it as tight as you choose, and he will not mind it.

You should see that the pad of your saddle is all right before you put it on, and that there is nothing to make it hurt him, or feel unpleasant to his back. It should not have any loose straps on the back part of it, to flap about and scare him. After you have saddled him in this way, take a switch in your right hand to tap him up with, and walk about in the stable a few times with your right arm over your saddle, taking hold of the reins on each side of his neck with your right and left hands, thus marching him about in the stable until you teach him the use of the bridle, and can turn him about in any direction, and stop him by a gentle pull of the rein. Always caress him, and loose the reins a little every time you stop him.

You should always be alone, and have your colt in some light stable or shed the first time you ride him; the loft should be high, so that you can sit on his back without endangering your head. You can teach him more in two hours' time in a stable of this kind than you could in two weeks in the common way of breaking colts, out in an open place. If you follow my course of treatment, you need not run any risk, or have any trouble in riding the worst kind of horse. You take him a step at a time, until you get up a mutual confidence and trust between yourself and horse. First teach him to lead and stand hitched; next acquaint him with the saddle and the use of the bit; and then, all that remains is, to get on him without scaring him, and you can ride him as well as any horse.

How to Mount the Colt.

First gentle him well on both sides, about the saddle, and all over, until he will stand still without holding, and is not afraid to see you anywhere about him.

As soon as you have him thus gentled, get a small block, about one foot or eighteen inches in height, and set it down by the side of him, about where you want to stand to mount him; step up on this, raising yourself very gently: horses notice every change of position very closely, and if you were to step up suddenly on the block, it would be very apt to scare him; but, by raising yourself gradually on it, he will see you, without being frightened, in a position very nearly the same as when you are on his back.

As soon as he will bear this without alarm, untie the stirrup-strap next to you, and put your left foot into the stirrup, and stand square over it, holding your knee against the horse, and your toe out, so as to touch him under the shoulder with the toe of your boot. Place your right hand on the front of the saddle, and on the opposite side of you, taking hold of a portion of the mane and the reins, as they hang loosely over his neck, with your left hand; then gradually bear your weight on the stirrup, and on your right hand, until the horse feels your whole weight on the saddle: repeat this several times, each time raising yourself a little higher from the block, until he will allow you to raise your leg over his croup and place yourself in the saddle.

There are three great advantages in having a block to mount from. First, a sudden change of position is very apt to frighten a young horse who has never been handled: he will allow you to walk up to him, and stand by his side, without scaring at you, because you have gentled him to that position; but if you get down on your hands and knees, and crawl towards him, he will be very much frightened; and upon the same principle he would be frightened at your new position, if you had the power to hold yourself over his back without touching him. Then the first great advantage of the block is to gradually gentle him to that new position in which he will see you when you ride him.

Secondly, by the process of leaning your

weight in the stirrups, and on your hand, you can gradually accustom him to your weight, so as not to frighten him by having him feel it all at once. And, in the third place, the block elevates you so that you will not have to make a spring in order to get on the horse's back, but from it you can gradually raise yourself into the saddle. When you take these precautions, there is no horse so wild but what you can mount him without making him jump. I have tried it on the worst horses that could be found, and have never failed in any case. When mounting, your horse should always stand without being held. A horse is never well broken when he has to be held with a tight rein when mounting; and a colt is never so safe to mount as when you see that assurance of confidence, and absence of fear, which cause him to stand without holding.

How to Ride the Colt.

When you want him to start, do not touch him on the side with your heel, or do anything to frighten him and make him jump. But speak to him kindly, and if he does not start, pull him a little to the left until he starts, and then let him walk off slowly with the reins loose. Walk him around in the stable a few times until he gets used to the bit, and you can turn him about in every direction, and stop him as you please. It would be well to get on and off a good many times, until he gets perfectly used to it before you take him out of the stable.

After you have trained him in this way, which should not take you more than one or two hours, you can ride him anywhere you choose without ever having him jump or make an effort to throw you.

When you first take him out of the stable, be very gentle with him, as he will feel a little more at liberty to jump or run, and be a little easier frightened than he was while in the stable. But after handling him so much in the stable, he will be pretty well broken, and you will be able to manage him without trouble or danger.

When you first mount him take a little the shortest hold on the left rein, so that if anything frightens him you can prevent him from jumping by pulling his head around to you. This operation of pulling a horse's head round against his side will prevent any horse from jumping ahead, rearing up, or running away. If he is stubborn and will not go, you can make him move by pulling his head round to one side, when whipping would have no effect. And turning him round a few times will make him dizzy, and then by letting him have his head straight, and giving him a little touch with the whip, he will go along without any trouble.

Never use martingales on a colt when you first ride him; every movement of the hand should go right to the bit in the direction in which it is applied to the reins, without a martingale to change the direction of the force applied. You can guide the colt much better without it, and teach him the use of the bit in much less time. Besides, martingales would prevent you from pulling his head round if he should try to jump.

After your colt has been ridden until he is gentle and well accustomed to the bit, you may find it an advantage if he carries his head too high, or his nose too far out, to put martingales on him.

You should be careful not to ride your colt so far at first as to heat, worry, or tire him. Get off as soon as you see he is a little fatigued; gentle him and let him rest; this will make him kind to you and prevent him from getting stubborn or mad.

―――――

THE PROPER WAY TO BIT A COLT.

Farmers often put a bitting harness on a colt the first thing they do to him, buckling up the bitting as tight as they can draw it, to make him carry his head high, and then turn him out in a field to run a half-day at a time. This is one of the worst punishments that they could inflict on the colt, and very injurious to a young horse that has been used to running in pasture with his head down. I have seen colts so injured in this way that they never got over it.

A horse should be well accustomed to the bit before you put on the bitting harness, and when you first bit him you should only rein his head up to that point where he naturally holds it, let that be high or low; he will soon learn that he cannot lower his head, and that raising it a little will loosen the bit in his mouth. This will give him the idea of raising his head to loosen the bit, and then you can draw the bitting a little tighter every time you put it on, and he will still raise his head to loosen it; by this means you will gradually get his head and neck in the position you want him to carry it, and give him a nice and graceful carriage without hurting him, making him mad, or causing his mouth to get sore.

If you put the bitting on very tight the first time, he cannot raise his head enough to loosen it, but will bear on it all the time, and paw, sweat, and throw himself. Many horses have been killed by falling backward with the bitting on; their heads being drawn up strike the ground with the whole weight of the body.

MR. RAREY'S EXTRA STRAP.

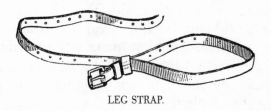

LEG STRAP.

Horses that have their heads drawn up tightly should not have the bitting on more than fifteen or twenty minutes at a time.

How to Drive a Horse That Is Very Wild and Has Any Vicious Habits.

Take up one fore foot and bend his knee till his hoof is bottom upwards, and nearly touching his body; then slip a loop over his knee, and up until it comes above the pastern joint, to keep it up, being careful to draw the loop together between the hoof and pastern joint with a second strap of some kind to prevent the loop from slipping down and coming off. This will leave the horse standing on three legs; you can now handle him as you wish, for it is utterly impossible for him to kick in this position. There is something in this operation of taking up one foot that conquers a horse quicker and better than anything else you can do to him. There is no process in the world equal to it to break a kicking horse, for several reasons. First, there is a principle of this kind in the nature of the horse: that by conquering one member you conquer to a great extent the whole horse.

You have perhaps seen men operate upon this principle, by sewing a horse's ears together to prevent him from kicking. I once saw a plan given in a newspaper to make a bad horse stand to be shod, which was to fasten down one ear. There were no reasons given why you should do so; but

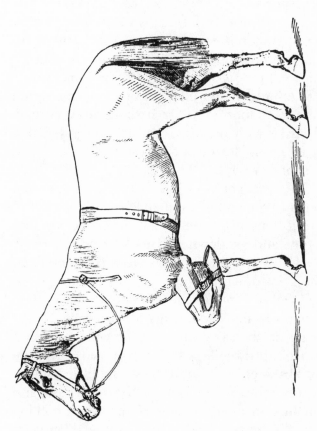

THE HORSE WITH LEG STRAP AND SURCINGLE ON.

I tried it several times, and thought that it had a good effect—though I would not recommend its use; especially stitching his ears together. The only benefit arising from this process is, that by disarranging his ears we draw his attention to them, and he is not so apt to resist the shoeing. By tying up one foot we operate on the same principle to a much better effect. When you first fasten up a horse's foot he will sometimes get very mad, and strike with his knee, and try every possible way to get it down; but he cannot do that, and will soon give up.

This will conquer him better than anything you could do, and without any possible danger of hurting himself or you either, for you can tie up his foot and sit down and look at him until he gives up. When you find that he is conquered, go to him, let down his foot, rub his leg with your hand, caress him, and let him rest a little; then put it up again. Repeat this a few times, always putting up the same foot, and he will soon learn to travel on three legs so that you can drive him some distance. As soon as he gets a little used to this way of travelling, put on your harness, and hitch him to a sulky. If he is the worst kicking horse that ever raised a foot, you need not be fearful of his doing any damage while he has one foot up, for he cannot kick, neither can he run fast enough to do any harm. And if he is the wildest horse that ever had harness on, and has run away every time he has been hitched, you can now hitch him in a sulky, and drive him as you please. If he wants to run, you can let him have the lines, and the whip too, with perfect safety, for he can go but a slow gait on three legs, and will soon be tired, and willing to stop; only hold him enough to guide him in the right direction, and he will soon be tired and willing to stop at the word. Thus you will effectually cure him at once of any further notion of running off. Kicking horses have always been the dread of everybody; you always hear men say, when they speak about a bad horse, "I don't care what he does, so he don't kick." This new method is an effectual cure for this worst of all habits. There are plenty of ways by which you can hitch a kicking horse, and force him to go, though he kicks all the time; but this don't have any good effect towards breaking him, for we know that horses kick because they are afraid of what is behind them, and when they kick against it and it hurts them they will only kick the harder; and this will hurt them still more and make them remember the scrape much longer, and make it still more difficult to persuade them to have any confidence in anything dragging behind them ever after.

But by this new method you can hitch them to a rattling sulky, plough, wagon, or anything else in its worst shape. They may be frightened at first, but cannot kick or do anything to hurt themselves, and will soon find that you do not intend to hurt them, and then they will not care anything more about it. You can then let down the leg and drive along gently without any further trouble. By this new process a bad kicking horse can be learned to go gently in harness in a few hours' time.

On Balking.

Horses know nothing about balking, only as they are brought into it by improper management, and when a horse balks in harness it is generally from some mismanagement, excitement, confusion, or from not knowing how to pull, but seldom from any unwillingness to perform all that he understands. High-spirited, free-going horses are the most subject to balking, and only so because drivers do not properly understand how to manage this kind. A free horse in a team may be so anxious to go, that when he hears the word he will start with a jump, which will not move the load, but give him such a severe jerk on the shoulders that he will fly back and stop the other horse;

the teamster will continue his driving without any cessation, and by the time he has the slow horse started again he will find that the free horse has made another jump, and again flown back; and now he has them both badly balked, and so confused that neither of them knows what is the matter, or how to start the load. Next will come the slashing and cracking of the whip, and hallooing of the driver, till something is broken or he is through with his course of treatment. But what a mistake the driver commits by whipping his horse for this act! Reason and common sense should teach him that the horse is willing and anxious to go, but did not know how to start the load. And should he whip him for that? If so, he should whip him again for not knowing how to talk. A man that wants to act with any rationality or reason should not fly into a passion, but should always think before he strikes. It takes a steady pressure against the collar to move a load, and you cannot expect him to act with a steady, determined purpose while you are whipping him. There is hardly one balking horse in five hundred that will pull true from whipping; it is only adding fuel to the fire, and will make him more liable to balk another time. You always see horses that have been balked a few times, turn their heads and look back, as soon as they are a little frustrated.

This is because they have been whipped and are afraid of what is behind them. This is an invariable rule with balked horses, just as much as it is for them to look around at their sides when they have the bots; in either case they are deserving of the same sympathy and the same kind, rational treatment.

When your horse balks or is a little excited, if he wants to start quickly, or looks around and doesn't want to go — there is something wrong, and he needs kind treatment immediately. Caress him kindly, and if he doesn't understand at once what you want him to do, he will not be so much excited as to jump and break things, and do everything wrong through fear. As long as you are calm, and keep down the excitement of the horse, there are ten chances to have him understand you, where there would not be one under harsh treatment, and then the little flare up would not carry with it any unfavorable recollections, and he would soon forget all about it, and learn to pull true. Almost every wrong act the horse commits is from mismanagement, fear, or excitement; one harsh word will so excite a nervous horse as to increase his pulse ten beats in a minute.

When we remember that we are dealing with dumb brutes, and reflect how difficult it must be for them to understand our motions, signs, and language, we should never get out of patience with them because they don't understand us, or wonder at their doing things wrong. With all our intellect, if we were placed in the horse's situation, it would be difficult for us to understand the driving of some foreigner, of foreign ways and foreign language. We should always recollect that our ways and language are just as foreign and unknown to the horse as any language in the world is to us, and should try to practise what we could understand were we the horse, endeavoring by some simple means to work on his understanding rather than on the different parts of his body. All balked horses can be started true and steady in a few minutes' time; they are all willing to pull as soon as they know how, and I never yet found a balked horse that I could not teach to start his load in fifteen, and often less than three, minutes' time.

Almost any team, when first balked, will start kindly if you let them stand five or ten minutes as though there was nothing wrong, and then speak to them with a steady voice, and turn them a little to the right or left, so as to get them both in motion before they feel the pinch of the load. But if you want to start a team that you are not driving yourself, that has been balked, fooled and whipped for some time, go to them and hang the lines on their hames, or fasten them to the wagon, so that they will be perfectly loose; make the driver and spectators (if there are any) stand off some distance to one side, so as not to attract the attention of the horse; unloose their check-reins, so that they can get their heads down if they choose; let them stand a few minutes in this condition until you can see that they are a little composed. While they are standing you should be about their heads, gentling them; it will make them a little more kind, and the spectators will think that you are doing something that they do not understand, and will not learn the secret. When you have them ready to start, stand before them, and as you seldom have but one balky horse in a team, get as near in front of him as you can, and if he is too fast for the other horse, let his nose come against your breast; this will keep him steady, for he will go slow rather than run on you; turn them gently to the right, without letting them pull on the traces as far as the tongue will let them go; stop them with a kind word, gentle them a little, and then turn them back to the left, by the same process. You will have them under your control by this time, and as you turn them again to the right, steady them in the collar, and you can take them where you please.

There is a quicker process that will generally start a balky horse, but not so sure. Stand him a little ahead, so that his shoulders will be against the collar, and then take up one of his forefeet in your hand, and let the driver start them, and when the weight comes against his shoulders, he will try to step; then let him have his foot, and he will go right along. If you want to break a horse from balking that has long been in that habit, you ought to set apart a half-day for that purpose. Put him by the side of some steady horse; have check-lines on them; tie up all the traces and straps, so that there will be nothing to excite them; do not rein them up, but let them have their heads loose. Walk them about together for some time as slowly and lazily as possible; stop often, and go up to your balky horse and gentle him. Do not take any whip about him, or do any-thing to excite him, but keep him just as quiet as you can. He will soon learn to start off at the word, and stop whenever you tell him.

As soon as he performs rightly, hitch him in an empty wagon; have it stand in a favorable position for starting. It would be well to shorten the stay-chain behind the steady horse, so that if it is necessary, he can take the weight of the wagon the first time you start them. Do not drive but a few rods at first; watch your balky horse closely, and if you see that he is getting excited, stop him before he stops of his own accord, caress him a little, and start again. As soon as they go well, drive them over a small hill a few times, and then over a larger one, occasionally adding a little load.

This process will make any horse true to pull.

———

To Break a Horse to Harness.

Take him in a light stable, as you did to ride him; take the harness and go through the same process that you did with the saddle, until you get him familiar with it, so that you can put it on him, and rattle it about without his caring for it. As soon as he will bear this, put on the lines, caress him as you draw them over him, and drive him about in the stable till he will bear them over his hips. The lines are a great aggravation to some colts, and often frighten them as much as if you were to raise a whip over them. As soon as he is familiar with the harness and lines, take him out and put him by the side of a gentle horse, and go through the same process that you did with the balking horse. Always use a bridle without blinds when you are breaking a horse to harness.

How to Hitch a Horse in a Sulky.

Lead him to and around it; let him look at it, touch it with his nose, and stand by it till he does not care for it; then pull the shafts a little to the left, and stand your horse in front of the off-wheel. Let some one stand on the right side of the horse, and hold him by the bit, while you stand on the left side, facing the sulky. This will keep him straight. Run your left hand back, and let it rest on his hip, and lay hold of the shafts with your right, bringing them up very gently to the left hand, which still remains stationary. Do not let anything but your arm touch his back, and as soon as you have the shafts square over him, let the person on the opposite side take hold of one of them, and lower them very gently to the shaft-bearers. Be very slow and deliberate about hitching; the longer time you take the better, as a general thing. When you have the shafts placed, shake them slightly, so that he will feel them against each side. As soon as he will bear them without scaring, fasten your braces, etc., and start him along very slowly. Let one man lead the horse, to keep him gentle, while the other gradually works back with the lines till he can get behind and drive him. After you have driven him in this way a short distance, you can get into the sulky, and all will go right. It is very important to have your horse go gently when you first hitch him. After you have walked him awhile, there is not half so much danger of his scaring. Men do very wrong to jump up behind a horse to drive him as soon as they have him hitched. There are too many things for him to comprehend all at once. The shafts, the lines, the harness, and the rattling of the sulky, all tend to scare him, and he must be made familiar with them by degrees. If your horse is very wild, I would advise you to put up one foot the first time you drive him.

HOW TO MAKE A HORSE LIE DOWN.

Everything that we want to teach the horse must be commenced in some way to give him an idea of what you want him to do, and then be repeated till he learns it perfectly. To make a horse lie down, bend his left fore leg and slip a loop over it, so that he cannot get it down. Then put a surcingle around his body, and fasten one end of a long strap around the other fore leg, just above the hoof. Place the other end under

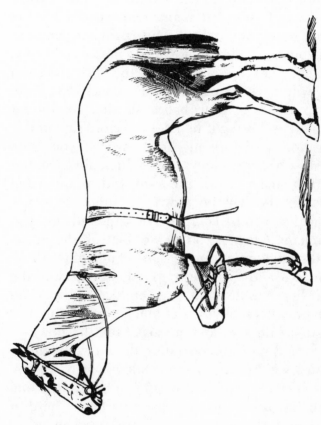

HORSE WITH MR. RAREY'S EXTRA STRAP ON.

the surcingle, so as to keep the strap in the right direction; take a short hold of it with your right hand; stand on the left side of the horse, grasp the bit in your left hand, pull steadily on the strap with your right; bear against his shoulder till you cause him to move. As soon as he lifts his weight, your pulling will raise the other foot, and he will have to come on his knees. Keep the strap tight in your hand, so that he cannot straighten his leg if he rises up. Hold him in this position, and turn his head towards you; bear against his side with your shoulder, not hard, but with a steady, equal pressure, and in about ten minutes he will lie down. As soon as he lies down, he will be completely conquered, and you can handle him as you please. Take off the straps, and straighten out his legs; rub him lightly about the face and neck with your hand the way the hair lies; handle all his legs, and after he has lain ten or twenty minutes, let him get up again. After resting him a short time make him lie down as before. Repeat the operation three or four times, which will be sufficient for one lesson. Give him two lessons a day, and when you have given him four lessons, he will lie down by taking hold of one foot. As soon as he is well broken to lie down in this way, tap him on the opposite leg with a stick when you take hold of his foot, and in a few days he will lie down from the mere motion of the stick.

How to Make a Horse Follow You.

Turn him into a large stable or shed, where there is no chance to get out, with a halter or bridle on. Go to him and gentle him a little, take hold of his halter and turn him towards you, at the same time touching him lightly over the hips with a long whip. Lead him the length of the stable, rubbing him on the neck, saying in a steady tone of voice as you lead him, "Come along boy?" or use his name instead of "boy" if you choose. Every time you turn touch him slightly with the whip, to make him step up close to you, and then caress him with your hand. He will soon learn to hurry up to escape the whip and be caressed, and you can make him follow you around without taking hold of the halter. If he should stop and turn from you, give him a few sharp cuts about the hind legs, and he will soon turn his head towards you, when you must always caress him. A few lessons of this kind will make him run after you, when he sees the motion of the whip—in twenty or thirty minutes he will follow you about the stable. After you have given him two or three lessons in the stable, take him out into a small field and train him; and from thence you can take him into the road and make him follow you anywhere, and run after you.

———

How to Make a Horse Stand without Holding.

After you have him well broken to follow you, place him in the center of the stable—begin at his head to caress him, gradually working backwards. If he moves, give him a cut with the whip, and put him back to the same spot from which he started. If he stands, caress him as before, and continue gentling him in this way until you can get round him without making him move. Keep walking around him, increasing your pace, and only touch him occasionally. Enlarge your circle as you walk around, and if he then moves, give him another cut with the whip, and put him back to his place. If he stands, go to him frequently and caress him, and then walk around him again. Do not keep him in one position too long at a time, but make him come to you occasionally, and follow you around the stable. Then make him stand in another place, and proceed as before. You should not train your horse more than half an hour at a time.

OTHER APPLEWOOD TITLES
YOU WILL ENJOY

The Emigrants' Guide to Oregon and California
LANSFORD W. HASTINGS

Published in 1845, this guidebook for pioneers is a
reproduction of one of the most collectible books about
California and the Western movement. It was the
guidebook used by the Donner Party on their fateful
journey. In addition, because Hastings' "shortcut" route
through the Rockies produced such tragedy, the War
Department commissioned *The Prairie Traveler.*
5⅜ x 8¼, 152 pp., $9.95

The Prairie Traveler
RANDOLPH B. MARCY

Filled with helpful information that was essential
for safe travel west as well as a fascinating view of
the strenuous life faced by prairie travelers
before the era of the railroad.
4¾ x 7⅛, 288 pp., $10.95

Songs of the Cowboys
N. HOWARD "JACK" THORP

This was the first cowboy songbook published in
America, and Thorp's lyrics were the beginning of the
popularization of the American cowboy. This book lists
24 songs that can be learned and sung today.
4½ x 7¼, 50 pp., $7.95

—— APPLEWOOD BOOKS ——
18 North Road, Bedford, MA 01730